Dedicated to all the love
with helping me find my bonnets.

Where Is My Bonnet?

ISBN-13: 978-0-692-02756-1
ISBN-10: 0-692-02756-4

Where Is My Bonnet?

Written and Illustrated by
Laura Shephard

"Time for bed."
That's what Mama said.

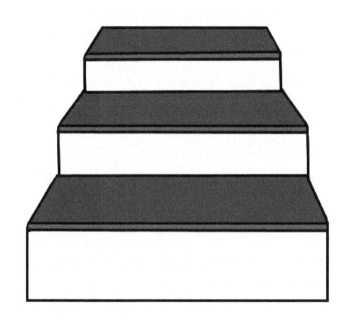

I rushed up the stairs
to get my special cloth
to wrap my curly hair.

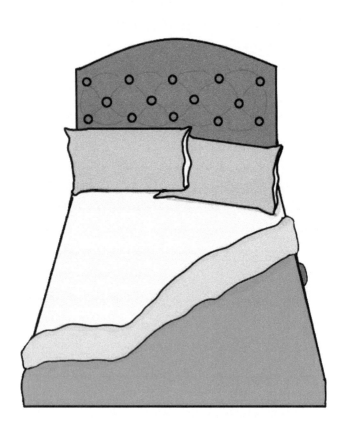

I looked under my cover,
but it was not there.

I asked my brother,
but he did not care.

Where is my bonnet?

"It's time for bed."
That's what Mama said.
I need to find my
special cloth
to wrap my coiled hair.

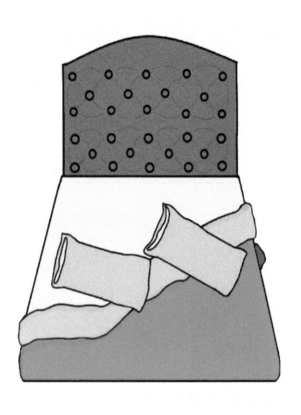

I looked under my pillows.

I asked my Grandma
Willow.

I emptied my barrette
caboodle.

I asked my poodle.

Where is my bonnet?

"It is time for bed!"
That's what Mama said.
I need to find my
special cloth
to wrap my kinky hair.

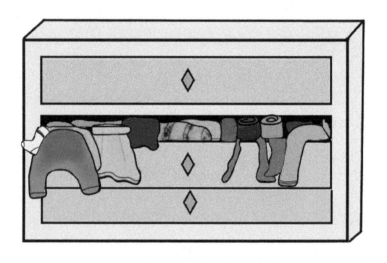

I looked in my drawer.

I looked behind my door.

I looked in my hamper.

I asked my hamster.

Where is my bonnet?

"Nia! Get ready for bed.
It's getting late.
Time to rest your head."

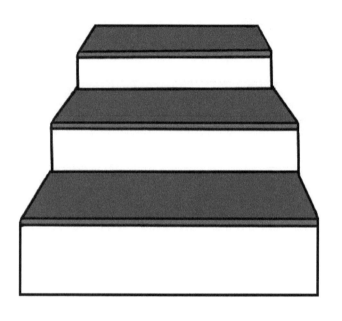

I stomped up the stairs.

I can't find my special
cloth to wrap my spongy
hair.

I said sorry to my hamster.

I put my dirty clothes in the hamper.

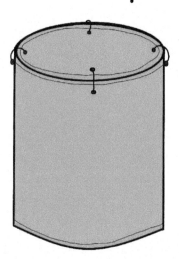

I cleaned behind the door.

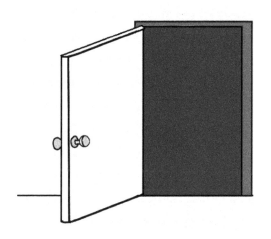

I put my clothes in the drawer.

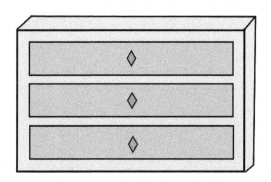

I pet my poodle.

I put my barrettes in
the caboodle.

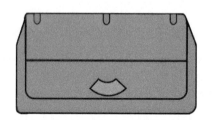

I kissed my Grandma Willow.

I fixed my pillows.

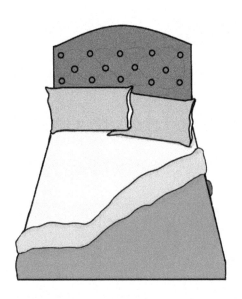

I said goodnight to my brother.

I said "I love you" to my mother.

I was about to lay my
head down when
suddenly...

I found it!

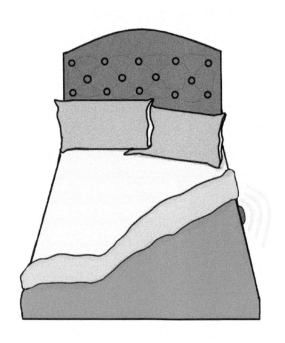

My satin bonnet was
under my bed!

Now I have my special
cloth

to wrap my special hair!

The End.

9 780692 027561